SHONEN JUMP'S
Yu-Gi-Oh!
ENTER THE SHADOW REALM
MONSTER DUEL
OFFICIAL HANDBOOK

D0201772

SCHOLASTIC INC.

New York   Toronto   London   Auckland   Sydney
Mexico City   New Delhi   Hong Kong   Buenos Aires

© 1996 Kazuki Takahashi

YU-GI-OH!

In ancient Egypt, there existed a force so powerful that it had to be locked away for a millennium. Now one boy has released that power.

It's time to duel!

According to legend, five thousand years ago the ancient Egyptian Pharaohs played a game called the Shadow Game. The game involved magical ceremonies, which were used to foresee the future and ultimately decide one's destiny. This game pitted *real* monsters against each other in brutal combat! With so many magical spells and ferocious creatures occupying the entire world, it wasn't long before a being truly evil and uncontrollable was brought back to life. Fortunately, a brave Pharaoh stepped in and averted disaster with the help of seven powerful magical artifacts.

Now the game has been revived in the form of the modern game, Duel Monsters. Duel Monsters is a card-battling game where players pit different mystical creatures against one another in wild, magical duels! The game is packed with awesome monsters and mighty spell-cards. However, these monsters aren't real; they're just images on playing cards.

Or are they?

YUGI

Yugi is a shy freshman at Domino High School who loves to play Duel Monsters. He is taught how to play by his grandfather, who also has a love for the game. Grandpa teaches him about the heart of the cards and how one must play with honor as well as skill. Yugi learns that even though he duels against his opponents, once the game is over, they can be friends. Yugi believes in his ability to overcome his adversaries and duels fairly no matter how underhanded some opponents may be.

One day, Grandpa gives Yugi an ancient Egyptian artifact called the Millennium Puzzle. Legend has it that whoever solves the puzzle will be granted dark and mysterious powers. The mysterious artifact captivates young Yugi.

Yugi tries and tries and eventually solves the mysterious Millennium Puzzle. However, when he does, something amazing happens! The puzzle instills Yugi with the spirit of an Egyptian Pharaoh. When their two souls merge into one, they become Yami Yugi! The Pharaoh's powerful spirit helps Yugi gain strength and confidence, allowing him to overcome obstacles and make new friends.

THE MILLENNIUM PUZZLE

GRANDPA

Yugi's grandfather owns the neighborhood gaming shop. He's a former world traveler who knows everything there is to know about games. He is especially well versed in the ways of Yugi's favorite game, Duel Monsters.

YAMI YUGI

Yami Yugi is full of confidence and courage. He is a master duelist who duels with honor and does not cheat. Through the help of Yami Yugi, young Yugi is slowly building confidence and self esteem himself.

The link between Yugi and Yami Yugi is the mystifying Millennium Puzzle. While Yugi may not know the full extent of the puzzle's power, he's slowly discovering its mysterious links to ancient Egypt.

MONSTER QUIZ #1

This monster slashed at its opponent with bony tusks!

YUGI'S MONSTERS

Yugi has a host of fierce and diverse monsters. Some more powerful than others, the true strength of Yugi's monster collection doesn't lie in the monsters themselves, but in how he plays them.

SUMMONED SKULL

Although not the brightest of monsters, Summoned Skull's primary weapon, electric shock, is brutal!

BEAVER WARRIOR

With his spiked armor, this rodent warrior can't be underestimated.

ALPHA THE MAGNET WARRIOR

Uses magnetic power to attack his enemies. As with any other magnet, he can also be combined with other Magnet Warriors.

YU-GI-OH! QUIZ #1

_____ is Seto Kaiba's younger brother.

9

BERFOMET

How does a flying monster with four arms grab you? Any way he wants!

BETA THE MAGNET WARRIOR

When Alpha the Magnet Warrior, Beta the Magnet Warrior, and Gamma the Magnet Warrior are combined, they form Valkyrion the Magna Warrior and reveal its true powers!

MONSTER QUIZ #2

His enormous shield protected his fellow monsters!

BIG SHIELD GARDNA

He may not be much on attacks, but for defense . . . well, let's just say they don't call him "big shield" for nothing!

BLACK LUSTER SOLDIER

Spectators are amazed by the swordsmanship of this fierce yet elegant knight.

11

CATAPULT TURTLE

This turtle uses monsters as bullets—weakening its enemies with each shot fired!

BUSTER BLADER

It takes a powerful warrior to wield a sword bigger than himself and slay dragons!

B. SKULL DRAGON

The result of Red-Eyes B. Dragon and Summoned Skull merging into one. Watch out!

CELTIC GUARDIAN

A steadfast warrior, the Guardian doesn't mind being the first on the battlefield.

YU-GI-OH! QUIZ #2

Yami Marik draws great power from the _____ _____.

CHIMERA THE FLYING MYTHICAL BEAST

This creature keeps opponents guessing with attacks coming from one of its two heads or its long snake-like tale!

DARK MAGICIAN

Summoning dark powers, this magician casts powerful spells over his enemies.

DARK MAGICIAN GIRL

Dark Magician Girl's spells are not to be taken lightly. She's learned everything she knows from her master, the Dark Magician.

DARK SAGE

He is the most powerful magician, having trained himself for thousands of years.

MONSTER QUIZ #3

This wolf sprang into battle with a ferocious growl!

EXODIA THE FORBIDDEN ONE

The guardian god for the ancient Egyptian palace, he's not to be taken lightly.

FERAL IMP

When playful fiends such as this enter the battlefield, it's bad news for anyone who has to face them.

GAIA THE FIERCE KNIGHT

Riding his trusty steed, Gaia needs no shield as he battles with two powerful lances!

GAIA THE DRAGON CHAMPION

This powerful knight is even stronger when riding the fierce Curse of Dragon!

YU-GI-OH! QUIZ #3

Joey Wheeler travels to the Duelist Kingdom to save his sister's

_____.

GAMMA THE MAGNET WARRIOR

Combined with the two other Magnet Warriors, this warrior fights with fury!

GIANT SOLDIER OF STONE

This mighty giant battles with literally tons of raw power and fury!

HORN IMP

All this fiend needs for battle is its single horn!

KURIBOH

He may look cute and cuddly, but this monster is full of surprises.

MONSTER QUIZ #4

This powerful magician can cause chaos and destruction for any foe.

MAGICIAN OF BLACK CHAOS

Monsters everywhere fear this powerful magician!

MAMMOTH GRAVEYARD

No bag-o'-bones here! This monster charges at opponents with its long, sharp tusks!

MYSTICAL ELF

Peaceful by nature, this spiritual creature defends much better than she attacks.

SILVER FANG

No collar or leash can restrain this ferocious canine!

YU-GI-OH! QUIZ # 4

Yami Yugi draws his power from the _____ _____.

WINGED DRAGON, GUARDIAN OF THE FORTRESS #1

Terror strikes from above when this dragon swoops in to assault the enemy!

VALKYRION THE MAGNA WARRIOR

When the power of three Magnet Warriors are combined, you get one very powerful monster!

MONSTER QUIZ #5

Riding his Curse of Dragon, this knight swooped into battle!

MAXIMILLION PEGASUS

Maximillion Pegasus created Duel Monsters, modeling it after the ancient Egyptian Shadow Game. Sophisticated and cultured, Pegasus seems to be a perfect gentleman. However, Pegasus has many dark secrets and his true objectives are unknown. He has replaced his left eye with an ancient Egyptian artifact called the Millennium Eye, an artifact that gives him strange and magical powers, including the ability to read other people's minds.

Pegasus forces Yugi to duel him in the mysterious Shadow Realm, where all the monsters and magic are real. Since Pegasus controls the game of the shadow, Yugi loses the duel. And in return Pegasus claims Grandpa's soul as his prize!

Yugi is then drawn into a Duel Monster's competition that Pegasus arranges. Yugi must duel his way through the tournament and defeat Pegasus in order to save his grandfather. The tournament is held in the Duelist Kingdom, where a supreme system of three dimensional images can be projected—making the battles seem all too real!

THE MILLENNIUM EYE

YU-GI-OH! QUIZ #5
Duel Monsters is a reincarnation of an ancient game called the
_____ Game.

MAXIMILLION'S MONSTERS

Some of Maximillion's monsters may seem innocent and harmless at first, but never judge a book by its cover. Maximillion Pegasus holds some of the most powerful monster cards in existence. Nobody knows just how many monsters Maximillion has, and he likes it that way.

BLUE-EYES TOON DRAGON

This small dragon has deceiving strength and dexterity. He is certainly one to keep an eye on.

DARK RABBIT

This rabbit won't invite you to a fun tea party. When he leaps into battle, there's nothing fun about it.

MONSTER QUIZ #6

This monster launched another monster into the air.

DRAGON PIPER

What magical spells will flow from this piper's flute?

MANGA RYU-RAN

Newly hatched, this "baby" dragon was born with plenty of power and giant stomping feet!

PARROT DRAGON

When his beak snaps shut, he tries to snatch more than just a tasty cracker!

RELINQUISHED

With his puzzling body, this creature keeps his opponent guessing about upcoming attacks!

YU-GI-OH! QUIZ #6

_____ _____ draws his dark power from the Millennium Ring._

RYU-RAN

Another young
dragon, he, too,
was born with
more strength than
most grown dragons.

THOUSAND-
EYES RESTRICT

Any opposing monster
will feel weak at the
knees when stared
at by this beast's
thousands of eyes.

TOON MERMAID

She may look cute and harmless but if you're careless, she'll hit you with a barrage of deadly arrows!

TOON SUMMONED SKULL

Who knew that summoning toons could be so powerful? You will, after your monsters face this beast.

MONSTER QUIZ # 7

The chains on this beast didn't slow him down!

JOEY WHEELER

Once a tough street kid, and a bully for young Yugi, Joey has learned the value of friendship. He has come to respect Yugi and become his loyal companion. Although sometimes Joey's harsh street background makes him quarrelsome and quick to act before he thinks, he has a kind heart and would do anything for his friends.

Joey joins Yugi in the Duelist Kingdom in hopes of winning the prize and saving his sister's eyesight.

JOEY'S MONSTERS

Joey holds some very powerful monster cards himself. His favorite is the Time Wizard—a card Yugi gave him as a symbol of friendship.

YU-GI-OH! QUIZ #7

The most powerful monster card is Marik's

_____ _____ _____.

ALLIGATOR'S SWORD

Using spiked armor for defense, Alligator's Sword slashes with his razor-sharp namesake.

ALLIGATOR'S SWORD DRAGON

This warrior's personal dragon gracefully carries him into combat!

AXE RAIDER

A slicing double-headed axe is this monster's weapon of choice!

BABY DRAGON

Baby Dragons learn to spit deadly fire before they can even walk!

MONSTER QUIZ # 8

The ground shook as his boulder-like feet stepped onto the dueling field.

BATTLE STEER

As it wields a lethal trident, no cowboy can tame this steer!

BATTLE WARRIOR

Spiked gloves add an ___ "punch" to this fi___ blows!

YU-GIOH! QUIZ #8

In the _____ Realm, all the monsters are real.

FLAME SWORDSMAN

The power of fire fuels this swordsman's mighty weapon!

GAROOZIS

Not of this world, deadly Garoozis carries a double-bladed battle-axe into battle!

MONSTER QUIZ # 9

He didn't build a dam. Instead, this rodent scurried into battle!

GEARFRIED THE IRON KNIGHT

This knight was skillfully trained to use his weapons as extensions of his own body—literally!

JINZO

Shooting powerful beams of energy, no competitor wants to fall under the deadly gaze of Jinzo!

PANTHER WARRIOR

Part feline, part human, this vicious warrior truly has cat-like reflexes!

RED-EYES B. DRAGON

Slashing claws, swiping tail, snapping jaws—all tools of the trade for this mighty dragon.

ROCKET WARRIOR

He may be tiny, but this warrior really blasts off and flies into battle!

SWAMP BATTLEGUARD

This monster uses his spiked club to bash and smash anything that moves!

SWORDSMAN OF LANDSTAR

Although a bit comical, this warrior displays some of the finest swordsmanship on the dueling field.

THOUSAND DRAGON

It's hard to tell what's worse, this dragon's powerful claws or its toxic breath.

YU-GI-OH! QUIZ # 9

*Among all of Yugi's friends,
_____ is often the voice of reason.*

41

TIGER AXE

Another feline warrior, Tiger Axe slashes at opponents with raw power and wild fury!

TIME WIZARD

Sometimes there is no greater weapon than time itself!

TÉA GARDNER

Téa was a childhood friend of Yugi's and, among all of his friends, is often the voice of reason. She is the biggest cheerleader in the group, always encouraging everyone to believe in themselves and to never give up. Téa loves her friends dearly and is willing to help them in any way she can.

MONSTER QUIZ # 10

She cast a dark spell on the competition.

43

TRISTAN TAYLOR

Tristan doesn't duel, but he likes to watch his friends Joey and Yugi battle monsters against their opponents. He and Joey are best friends, and although they bicker once in awhile, they always cover each other's backs. Sometimes Tristan is quick to panic, but when it comes down to it, he is willing to do whatever it takes to support and cheer on his friends.

MAI VALENTINE

As one of the top duelists in the world, Mai is as pretty as she is dangerous.

She's stylish and frequently self absorbed, but not above using her charm to advance her situation. Though she plays for superficial reasons, Mai is slowly learning from Yugi's example.

YU-GI-OH! QUIZ #10

_____ _____ invented the game Duel Monsters.

MAI'S MONSTERS

Mai's collection of monsters reflects Mai herself—dangerous women!

AMAZONESS FIGHTER

Amazons are some of the most powerful warriors in the world. And this warrior is no exception, as she uses brute force to overpower her enemies!

AMAZONESS SWORDSWOMAN

A finely honed sword is the weapon of choice for this Amazon.

AMAZONESS CHAIN MASTER

This warrior extends her strikes with a long, spiked chain!

MONSTER QUIZ # 11

Watch out for his deadly gaze!

HARPIE'S PET DRAGON

The only trick this pet does is battle opponents with its jagged claws and teeth.

HARPIE LADY SISTERS

These three sisters are very close. They are so close that they fight as one and leave opponents few choices for attacks and defenses.

SETO KAIBA

Seto Kaiba is the wealthy CEO of his own multinational high-tech corporation, KaibaCorp. However, his real passions lie in the world of Duel Monsters. There, he uses his ruthless business drive to overcome any and all who challenge him.

Kaiba is a master duelist who used to believe that card gaming was all about power. Kaiba thinks of Yugi as his rival, and his goal is to defeat Yugi. But with time will Kaiba learn about honor from Yugi and his friends?

YU-GI-OH! QUIZ # 11

_____ is the guardian of the Millennium items.

KAIBA'S MONSTERS

Seto Kaiba prides himself on collecting some of the most powerful monsters out there. He always wants more and, just like in the business world, he usually gets what he wants.

JUDGE MAN

He may be small, but Judge Man leaps at opponents with a fearsome spiked mace in each hand!

MONSTER QUIZ #12

The jackpot is deadly no matter how the numbers land.

HITOTSU-ME GIANT

That's right! Him giant! Him very strong! Him smash other monsters to bits!

BATTLE OX

Battle Ox uses his mighty battle-axe to slash and chop his way to victory!

BLUE-EYES ULTIMATE DRAGON

She is the ultimate dragon because she has three ferocious heads, each full of razor-sharp teeth!

YU-GI-OH! QUIZ # 12

Yugi and his friends attend _____ High School.

BLUE-EYES WHITE DRAGON

One of the most powerful beasts on the dueling field, this aggressive dragon strikes with uncontrolled ferocity!

LA JINN THE MYSTICAL GENIE OF THE LAMP

The only wish this genie grants is a wish to be beaten on the dueling field!

RABID HORSEMAN

This monster gallops into battle and slashes at opponents with his large battle-axe!

MONSTER QUIZ # 13

Polly want a cracker?
Don't be fooled by this deadly dragon!

RUDE KAISER

With plenty of armor for protection, Rude Kaiser hacks away with two large blades firmly mounted on his wrists.

SAGGI THE DARK CLOWN

The only tricks this clown performs are ones of might, magic, and dark illusion!

YU-GI-OH! QUIZ #13

With the help of the _____ ____, Pegasus can read his opponent's mind.

SWORDSTALKER

Wicked confidence shows on this creature's face as he steps onto the dueling field, wielding his razor-sharp sword!

VORSE RAIDER

Known for his relentless fighting style and double-bladed staff, the Vorse Raider is not an opponent to be taken lightly.

MONSTER QUIZ # 14

They are three sisters who fight as one.

YAMI BAKURA AND HIS MONSTERS

Bakura is a school friend of Yugi's, and both have a shared passion for Duel Monsters. Yet, something is not quite right about Bakura. It could be the effect of the powerful Millennium Ring—a large medallion he wears on a chain around his neck. When the Millennium Ring activates, Bakura is filled with dark power and becomes Yami Bakura. Yugi would like nothing better than to free Bakura's soul from the grasp of the dark Millennium Ring.

THE MILLENNIUM RING

SEVEN-ARMED FIEND

With seven arms, this creature doesn't need weapons to challenge other monsters!

DARK NECROFEAR

A dark and powerful demon, she is the thing that nightmares are made of.

YAMI MARIK AND HIS MONSTERS

Marik Ishtar is Ishizu's brother. He is also the keeper of the Millennium Rod—an artifact that allows him to control the minds of his opponents. He has the most powerful monster there is—The Winged Dragon of Ra. Yami Marik will stop at nothing until he's added all of the god cards to his deck.

MAKYURA THE DESTRUCTOR

Other monsters are wary as this slashing creature steps onto the dueling field.

THE MILLENNIUM ROD

YU-GI-OH! QUIZ # 14

In the Duelist Kingdom, Yugi and his friends played for _____ _____.

THE MILLENNIUM KEY

THE MILLENNIUM SCALE

SHADI

Shadi is a mysterious Egyptian and little is known about his origins. He's also the guardian of the Millennium items and the owner of the Millennium Scale and Millennium Key.

MONSTER QUIZ # 15

It's difficult to fight when your monsters are surrounded by this creature's fog.

ISHIZU ISHTAR

Ishizu Ishtar, an Egyptian historian, is Marik's older sister. As the keeper of the Millennium Necklace she reveals the origins of the Duel Monster game.

THE MILLENNIUM NECKLACE

YU-GI-OH! QUIZ # 15

Grandpa taught Yugi about the _____ of the cards!

ARKANA AND HIS MONSTERS

Arkana is the magician duelist whose deck is full of the darkest of magic cards.

DARK MAGICIAN ARKANA

Look out! This dark magician's spells pack a powerful punch!

DOLL OF DEMISE

This is not a doll to be toyed with!

ODION AND HIS MONSTER

Odion was raised by Marik and Ishizu's parents in Egypt. Now he often does Marik's dirty work for him.

EMBODIMENT OF APOPHIS

The most evil of all Egyptian gods, this snake warrior now takes sword in hand to do battle!

MONSTER QUIZ # 16

This flying monster grows in power with each turn.

WEEVIL UNDERWOOD AND HIS MONSTERS

Weevil Underwood is a trickster! His web of cards is full of burrowing bugs.

GREAT MOTH

This monster flies across the dueling field as only a moth could.

INSECT QUEEN

A monster is severely punished if it doesn't bow down to this queen!

UMBRA AND LUMIS AND THEIR MONSTER

Umbra and Lumis are tag-team duelists.

MASKED BEAST GUARDIUS

Nobody wants to see what's behind this ferocious monster's mask!

YU-GI-OH! QUIZ #16

Ishizu uses the _____ _____ to see the future.

MAKO TSUNAMI AND HIS MONSTERS

Mako Tsunami is the sea duelist whose deck of cards is flooded with underwater beasts.

FIEND KRAKEN

All this monster wants to do is hug his opponents and squeeze them tightly.

MONSTER QUIZ #17

This guardian reflects all attacks.

FORTRESS WHALE

With a horn and gun turrets, this whale swims into any battle with complete confidence!

JELLYFISH

Not big on speed, this large sea creature will slowly sting an adversary with its hundreds of wispy tentacles.

KAIRYU-SHIN

This winged eel soars through the sky and bites at enemies from above!

BANDIT KEITH AND HIS MONSTERS

Bandit Keith is a cheat and a thief and plays with a vengeance.

LAUNCHER SPIDER

This spider launches explosive missiles at its enemies!

YU-GI-OH! QUIZ #17

_____ _____ controls an ocean of sea monsters.

PENDULUM MACHINE

Pendulum Machine is ready to slice the competition in half!

SLOT MACHINE

When you hit the jackpot on this slot machine, it's not a good thing.

MONSTER QUIZ # 18

This powerful monster really knows how to sting!

69

REX RAPTOR AND HIS MONSTERS

As the dinosaur duelist, Rex Raptor's deck is packed with mammoth monsters.

SWORD ARM OF DRAGON

From its protective spiked back to its sharp slashing tale, it's hard for an opponent to get close to this monster.

TWO-HEADED KING REX

This dragon is double the trouble as both heads bite all who come near!

PARADOX BROTHERS AND THEIR MONSTERS

The Paradox Brothers are identical twins who speak in rhyme. They are Pegasus's henchmen and guard the entrance to Pegasus's castle.

GATE GUARDIAN

Think twice before attacking this guardian, who reflects the best of attacks.

SHADOW GHOUL

Be very wary of those shadows!

YU-GI-OH! QUIZ #18

_____ - _____ _____

is Joey's favorite card.

BONZ AND HIS MONSTERS

Bonz's eerie deck is swarming with ghouls and zombies.

ARMORED ZOMBIE

The battle *never* ends for this ancient samurai warrior!

CLOWN ZOMBIE

This is what happens to a clown when he's down . . . and comes back as a zombie!

MONSTER QUIZ # 19

Be careful what you wish for with this mighty monster!

PANIK AND HIS MONSTER

Hired by Pegasus to defeat Yugi and his friends, Panik uses his Castle of Dark Illusions to surround all the monsters in a sea of dark mist and thereby forcing his opponents to fight hidden enemies.

CASTLE OF DARK ILLUSIONS

It is a fortress of impenetrable defense.

YU-GI-OH! QUIZ #19

The _____ _____ are twin henchmen who talk in rhyme.

THE WINGED DRAGON OF RA

This dragon's power is as strong as the Sun God, Ra, and he only listens to those who can speak the ancient Egyptian language.

SLIFER THE
SKY DRAGON

The endless power of
this dragon god brings
most monsters to
their knees!

OBELISK THE TORMENTOR

As his name suggests, this brutal god shows no mercy to any monster challenging him!

MONSTER MATCH!

These famous duelists haven't lost their monsters to one another in powerful duels. They're just out of order! Draw a line from the monster to the duelist who owns it!

MONSTER QUIZ # 20

Time's ticking away and so are your chances to escape from this monster.

77

Find Yugi's hidden message in the letters below by coloring in all the Bs, Fs, Gs, and Js!

JBALFWGAJJYSSHFOJGBWKIGNBDNBEJSS

TGRGUBSJFTABNBGDBRGGESJBPECBFGJT

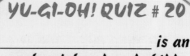

YU-GI-OH! QUIZ # 20

_____ is an
orphan/abandoned child.

ANSWERS

YU-GI-OH! QUIZZES

#1 – Mokuba

#2 – Millennium Rod

#3 – eyesight

#4 – Millennium Puzzle

#5 – Shadow

#6 – Yami Bakura

#7 – The Winged Dragon of Ra

#8 – Shadow

#9 – Téa

#10 – Maximillion Pegasus

#11 – Shadi

#12 – Domino

#13 – Millennium Eye

#14 – star chips

#15 – heart

#16 – Millennium Necklace

#17 – Mako Tsunami

#18 – Red-Eyes B. Dragon

#19 – Paradox Brothers

#20 – Odion

MONSTER QUIZZES

#1 – Mammoth Graveyard

#2 – Big Shield Gardna

#3 – Silver Fang

#4 – Magician of Black Chaos

#5 – Gaia the Dragon Champion

#6 – Catapult Turtle

#7 – Exodia the Forbidden One

#8 – Giant Solider of Stone

#9 – Beaver Warrior

#10 – Dark Magician Girl

#11 – Jinzo

#12 – Slot Machine

#13 – Parrot Dragon

#14 – Harpie Lady Sisters

#15 – Castle of Dark Illusions

#16 – Great Moth

#17 – Gate Guardian

#18 – Jellyfish

#19 – La Jinn the Mystical Genie of the Lamp

#20 – Time Wizard

ANSWERS
MONSTER MATCH!

SECRET MESSAGE!
Always show kindness, trust, and respect.